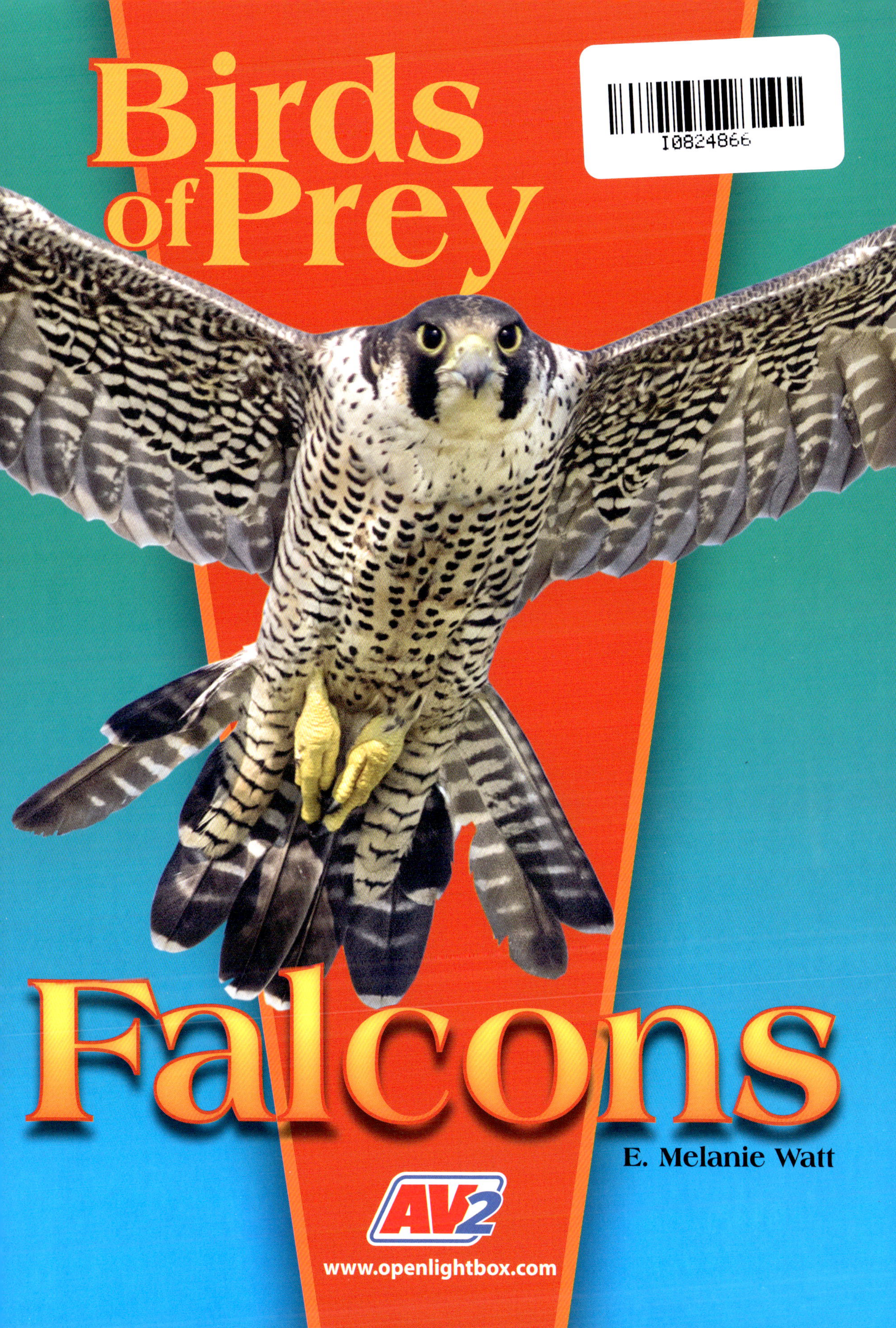
I0824866
Birds of Prey
Falcons
E. Melanie Watt
AV2
www.openlightbox.com

Step 1
Go to **www.openlightbox.com**

Step 2
Enter this unique code
ELHTSTRN2

Step 3
Explore your interactive eBook!

AV2 is optimized for use on any device

Your interactive eBook comes with...

Contents
Browse a live contents page to easily navigate through resources

Audio
Listen to sections of the book read aloud

Videos
Watch informative video clips

Weblinks
Gain additional information for research

Slideshows
View images and captions

Try This!
Complete activities and hands-on experiments

Key Words
Study vocabulary, and complete a matching word activity

Quizzes
Test your knowledge

Share
Share titles within your Learning Management System (LMS) or Library Circulation System

Citation
Create bibliographical references following the Chicago Manual of Style

This title is part of our AV2 digital subscription

1-Year K–5 Subscription
ISBN 978-1-7911-3320-7

Access hundreds of AV2 titles with our digital subscription.
Sign up for a FREE trial at **www.openlightbox.com/trial**

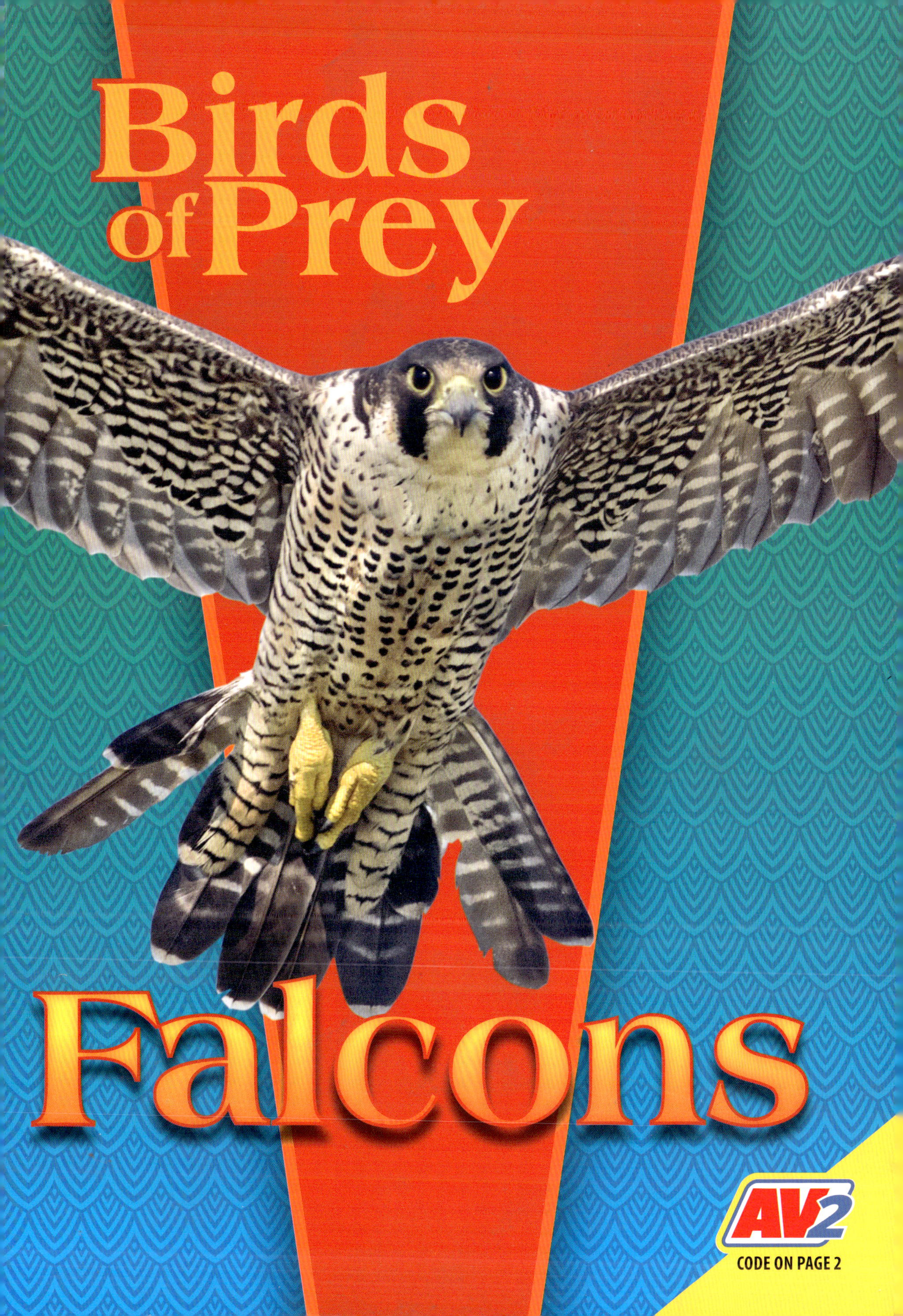
Birds of Prey
Falcons
AV2
CODE ON PAGE 2

Falcons

CONTENTS

Meet the Falcon

Falcons are part of a group of birds known as raptors, or birds of **prey**. Raptors hunt other animals for food. There are many types of birds of prey, including falcons, eagles, hawks, and owls. They all have curved beaks, strong eyesight, and sharp **talons**.

Compared to eagles and hawks, falcons tend to have smaller bodies. However, they have longer wings for their body size. This helps falcons fly and dive more quickly than both hawks and eagles. Falcons often hunt flying prey, catching birds and bats in the air.

Cool Facts

Falcons make several sounds. They use calls to communicate with mates or to defend food and territories. Falcons also chitter, creak, whine, wail, and "kak."

Types of Falcons

Although all falcon **species** share common features, they have a wide range of different shapes, colors, and sizes.

American Kestrel
(*Falco sparverius*)

Aplomado Falcon
(*Falco femoralis*)

Bat Falcon
(*Falco rufigularis*)

Gray Kestrel
(*Falco ardosiaceus*)

Laggar Falcon
(*Falco jugger*)

Merlin
(*Falco columbarius*)

Peregrine Falcon
(*Falco peregrinus*)

Red-Necked Falcon
(*Falco chicquera*)

Falcon Features

Falcons have many **adaptations** that help them find, chase, and kill their prey. These features include their sharp senses and the shape of their bodies.

WINGS
Falcons have long, thin wings with pointed tips. These allow the birds to fly quickly and maneuver easily in the air to snatch prey.

Falconry is a practice in which people train raptors, such as falcons, to hunt small animals. Ancient records show that falconry may have first been practiced more than 8,000 years ago.

FEET
Falcons have long toes with sharp talons. This helps them catch birds by grasping their prey's body through its feathers. Diving falcons also use their talons to stun or kill flying prey.

EYES
A falcon's eyesight is eight times better than a human's, allowing it to see small prey from almost 2 miles (3.2 kilometers) away.

BEAK
A falcon has a tooth-like shape on its upper bill and a matching empty space on its lower beak. These work like scissors to cut through meat.

BODY
A falcon's body is slender and streamlined. This helps it to move easily through the air when it dives after prey.

Size and Shape

Although falcons share similar features, they are not all the same. There are differences in **wingspan** and shape between the many falcon species. Differences exist within a falcon species as well. Male falcons tend to be about one-third smaller than females of the same species.

There are about 60 species of falcons in the world. These species are often divided into three or four groups. The first group, kestrels, is made up of small and stocky falcons. The second group includes slightly larger falcons, called hobbies, and their relatives. A third group of larger, more powerful falcons includes peregrine falcons and similar birds. Some members of this third group, known as hierofalcons, are sometimes placed in their own group. They are more vividly colored than peregrine falcons.

A male falcon is also known as a tiercel. Female falcons are always called falcons.

Falcon Wingspans

Seychelles Kestrel
Wingspan
Between 17 and 19 inches (43 and 48 centimeters)

American Kestrel
Wingspan
Between 20 and 24 inches (51 and 61 cm)

Red-Footed Falcon
Wingspan
Between 26 and 30 inches (66 and 76 cm)

Peregrine Falcon
Wingspan
Between 31 and 45 inches (79 and 114 cm)

Brown Falcon
Wingspan
Between 35 and 45 inches (89 and 114 cm)

Gyrfalcon
Wingspan
Between 43 and 48 inches (109 and 122 cm)

Falcon Habitats

Falcons are found throughout the world. They live on every continent except Antarctica. Falcons occupy many different types of **habitats**, including deserts, grasslands, tropical and temperate forests, wetlands, and **tundra**. Some species of falcons have also adapted to live in and around towns and cities. Within these habitats, falcons need to find food and mates, and raise their young.

Some species, such as the peregrine falcon, can be found in many places. Others are only found in certain habitats. Seychelles kestrels are only found on the islands of Seychelles in the West Indian Ocean. Some falcons **migrate** thousands of miles (km) to get to their preferred summer or winter habitats. Other species do not migrate at all.

Falcons do not all build nests. Instead, some use nests made by other birds. They may also live on cliffs, inside holes in trees, on the ground, or on buildings.

Amur falcons migrate great distances between East Asia and South Africa. They migrate in huge groups of thousands of birds.

Cool Facts

There are many names commonly used for a group of falcons. A group may be called a cast, a soar, or a tower.

Life Cycle

Falcons spend much of their time alone, except during breeding season. They **breed** once a year and stay with their mates to raise their young. Pairs may return to the same nest each year.

1 Eggs

The number and size of falcon eggs depends on the species. Female falcons usually lay two to four eggs. The male brings food while the female guards the nest and **incubates** the eggs. Falcon eggs hatch about one month after being laid.

2 Nestlings

A female falcon stays with her **nestlings** for the first 7 to 10 days after they hatch. She tears up prey into small pieces for the nestlings to eat. A month or more after hatching, the young falcons can fly and are no longer nestlings. However, they may continue to be fed by their parents for about eight weeks.

3 Adults

Once fully grown, a falcon will try to find a mate. Displays to attract a mate are mostly done by males. They include flying in loops or patterns. A male may also give a female gifts of food. Falcons tend to live to about 13 years in the wild, but some live up to 20. **Captive** falcons have lived well into their 20s.

What Do Falcons Eat?

Different falcon species each prefer to eat certain types of prey. Peregrine falcons and other large species usually eat medium-sized birds, along with other small or medium animals. Mid-sized species, such as hobbies, mostly eat insects or small birds. Kestrels tend to eat rodents, reptiles, and insects. Falcons may also steal food from other birds of prey.

Falcons hunt while flying. They either catch their prey in flight or snatch it from the ground. After they hunt, falcons often hide any extra food to eat later, sometimes storing it near their nest. Falcons use their beaks to pull meat from their prey. Sometimes, they consume things they cannot digest, such as bones or feathers. After the meat is digested, the other materials are coughed up in a clump called a pellet.

The peregrine falcon is thought to hunt thousands of different species of prey.

Several species of falcons, including some kestrels, are considered helpful to people. They eat mice, locusts, and other pests.

Falcons around the World

Falcons breed, hunt, and raise their young in many different habitats. This affects what they eat and how they hunt. Although falcons share similarities, they have unique behaviors that help them suit their homes.

PEREGRINE FALCON

Peregrine falcons are found all around the world. These birds are the fastest animals in the world. When hunting, they dive toward their prey at speeds that can reach 200 miles (320 km) per hour. The word *peregrine* means "wanderer." Some peregrines migrate between summer nests in the Arctic and South America. They fly up to 15,500 miles (25,000 km) each year. Others spend their lives in one place.

AMERICAN KESTREL

American kestrels are found in both North and South America. These birds are the smallest falcons in North America. They hover while hunting by using the wind, fast wing beats, and adjusting their tails to keep in one spot over a field. American kestrels prefer open areas with few trees. In many states, people build nest boxes for American kestrels. The birds return each spring to nest and raise their young in the boxes.

MERLIN

These small, fierce falcons are found across Europe, Asia, and North America. They mostly hunt small to medium-sized birds, catching their prey in the air in high-speed attacks. Sometimes, pairs of merlins work together to hunt. One scares a flock from below, while the other chases the birds until they tire. Merlin populations are stable or increasing, and the birds breed in many areas, including cities. There are about 3 million breeding merlins in the world.

GYRFALCON

The gyrfalcon is the world's largest falcon. These birds can be about 2 feet long (60 cm) and can weigh 4 pounds (1.8 kilograms). Gyrfalcons breed in Arctic regions, including northern Canada and Alaska. They prefer open areas where the birds they eat, such as ptarmigan, are common. Gyrfalcons may also hunt mammals such as hares. Gyrfalcon pairs mate for life. Males display in the air with impressive dives and rolls.

Falcon Encounters

Falcons may be smaller than many other birds of prey, but they can still be aggressive. They defend hunting territories around their nests. Falcons will also attack humans, pets, and other animals to protect their nests. Even if a falcon does not physically strike an intruder, these encounters waste the bird's energy and can put eggs or nestlings at risk when the falcon leaves its nest.

Many people want to view falcon eggs and nestlings up close, without disturbing the birds. To help people do this, webcams have been installed in falcon nests around the world. Webcams are easy to set up in falcon nests, as the birds often make their homes on buildings and in nest boxes.

Some airports use trained falcons to chase gulls and other birds away. This helps reduce collisions between aircraft and birds.

Peregrine falcons are commonly found in cities. Skyscrapers are similar to the cliffs on which the raptors normally nest. Additionally, there are many birds, such as pigeons, for them to hunt.

Protecting Falcons

Many falcon species are considered **endangered**, vulnerable, or near-threatened. The biggest threats to falcons come from people. These threats include hunting and the loss of habitat due to forests being cut down. Some people also steal falcon eggs or nestlings from their nests to use in falconry.

People have helped falcons by creating laws to protect them and their habitats. Conservation groups, such as the Peregrine Fund, have developed captive breeding programs. These help increase falcon numbers by releasing captive-bred birds into nature once they are grown.

The Peregrine Fund was established in 1970. Since then, it has raised more than 5,000 falcons, along with other raptors.

Peregrine Falcon Case Study

During the 1950s, many birds of prey, including peregrine falcons, were being poisoned by DDT, a chemical put on plants to kill insects. The falcons suffered when they ate birds that had eaten poisoned insects or plants. DDT weakened falcon eggshells, causing the eggs to break before they could hatch. Peregrines were placed on the U.S. Endangered Species List in 1970.

People worked hard to save the birds affected by DDT. In 1972, the United States banned the use of DDT. Captive breeding programs in the United States and Canada released 4,000 young birds into areas that once had peregrine falcons. By 1999, peregrine falcons were no longer endangered in the United States.

Falcon Quiz

1 What shape do falcons have on their upper bill?

2 How far can peregrine falcons travel in a year?

3 What is North America's smallest falcon species?

4 What speed can a peregrine falcon reach while diving?

5 What are three names for a group of falcons?

6 How can falcons help reduce collisions between birds and aircraft?

7 What is the largest falcon species?

8 Which falcon species migrates great distances between East Asia and South Africa?

Answers:
1. A tooth-like shape **2.** Up to 15,500 miles (25,000 km) **3.** The American kestrel
4. 200 miles (320 km) per hour **5.** A cast, a soar, or a tower **6.** By chasing away other birds
7. The gyrfalcon **8.** The Amur falcon

Key Words

adaptations: changes in animals that help them survive in their environment

breed: have young

captive: not living in a natural habitat

endangered: in danger of no longer existing anywhere on Earth

habitats: places where animals or plants normally live in nature

incubates: sits on eggs to keep them warm

migrate: travel a long distance when the seasons change

nestlings: birds too young to leave the nest

prey: animals that are hunted by other animals for food

species: a group of animals with the same characteristics; members of a species can usually only breed with other members of the same species

talons: sharp claws found on certain birds of prey

tundra: plains with small plants and frozen ground

wingspan: the width of a bird's wings, from tip to tip, when they are spread out

Index

Get the best of both worlds.

AV2 bridges the gap between print and digital.

The expandable resources toolbar enables quick access to content including **videos**, **audio**, **activities**, **weblinks**, **slideshows**, **quizzes**, and **key words**.

Animated videos make static images come alive.

Resource icons on each page help readers to further **explore key concepts**.

Published by Lightbox Learning Inc.
276 5th Avenue, Suite 704 #917
New York, NY 10001
Website: www.openlightbox.com

Library of Congress Control Number: 2022938946

ISBN 978-1-7911-4709-9 (hardcover)
ISBN 978-1-7911-4710-5 (softcover)
ISBN 978-1-7911-4711-2 (multi-user eBook)

Printed in Guangzhou, China
1 2 3 4 5 6 7 8 9 0 26 25 24 23 22

072022
101121

Project Coordinator: John Willis
Designer: Terry Paulhus

Photo Credits
Every reasonable effort has been made to trace ownership and to obtain permission to reprint copyright material. The publisher would be pleased to have any errors or omissions brought to its attention so that they may be corrected in subsequent printings. The publisher acknowledges Alamy, Minden Pictures, Newscom, Getty Images, and Shutterstock as its primary image suppliers for this title.

View new titles and product videos at www.openlightbox.com